THE DOUBLE BIRTHDAY PRESENT

THE DOUBLE BIRTHDAY PRESENT

BY

MABEL LEIGH HUNT

Illustrated by Elinore Blaisdell

J. B. LIPPINCOTT COMPANY
PHILADELPHIA AND NEW YORK

First Edition

PRINTED IN THE UNITED STATES OF AMERICA

TO

JEANNIE WRIGHT

Who loves to give birthday presents

THE FIRST CHAPTER

Sophie and Susie Gooding were twins. They looked almost exactly alike, and if you happened not to know them very well, it is likely you could not have said, right off, which was Susie, and which was Sophie.

But as their Grandpa Gooding sometimes pointed out to anyone who seemed puzzled, "If thee looks closely, thee will see that it's

Sophie who has the dimple in her cheek, while Susie—"

Then Grandpa Gooding would slip his arm gently around Susie, to comfort her.

Of course Susie knew, just by glancing at Sophie, that a dimple in a rosy, six-year-old cheek is quite a pretty adornment. It is undoubtedly nicer having one, than not. But the lack of a dimple didn't really bother Susie. For if you are a little Quaker girl like Susie, or like Sophie, you know far better than to spend your precious time thinking of your looks.

"Comb thy hair neatly. Scrub thy face. Keep thy clothing clean. Mind thy manners and improve thy mind and busy thy hands. Be thankful in thy heart for the gifts of earth and heaven. Think and speak and

act kindly. That is enough, let who may have dimples."

So said Grandpa Gooding, whenever he thought Sophie or Susie needed such advice.

"Too," added Rachel Gooding, who was the twins' mother, "there is something odd about a dimple in thy cheek. It doesn't show itself, at least not at its best, unless thee smiles."

Sophie's dimple showed itself almost all the time, because she was so happy being a twin. So was Susie happy. They never quarreled. In fact, they were much too busy having fun together, and with Grandpa Gooding, to heed so small a thing as a dimple. It was only a clever little trick of Nature's, so they had been told, for telling them apart.

3

THE SECOND CHAPTER

Grandpa Gooding was also a very happy person. Like Susie, he wore no dimple in his cheek as a sign of joy. So he whistled. He could not carry a tune, because neither his father, nor his grandfather, nor any of his Quaker ancestors could ever manage to carry a tune. But Grandpa Gooding whistled anyway. He whistled all the time, except when he was eating, sleeping, talking, or sitting in worship in the meeting-house on First Days.

"Why does thee whistle so much, Grandpa?" asked Susie.

Grandpa Gooding whistled very softly while he thought it over. "I think it's because I feel so blessed in having twin grand-daughters," he said. "They're right uncommon. 'Tisn't every grandpa has 'em. At least, not such well-behaved ones."

"Pshaw, Grandpa!" chided Sophie, dimpling, and smiling modestly. "I know the real reason thee whistles. It's because thee loves to work in thy cabinet shop. Thee dotes on making fine chairs and clocks and chests and tables that folks so admire to have."

"Yes, dear Grandpa, thy work and thy whistling go together," chimed Susie.

It was true that Grandpa Gooding whistled his merriest when he was working in

his cabinet shop. To spend long, pleasant weeks carving a beautiful clock that would tick the hours away for a hundred years and more; to put together, slowly and carefully, a handsome, tall-backed chair; to fashion a table of sound, fragrant wood, rubbing and polishing until every surface gleamed with its own richness—oh, indeed, Grandpa Gooding loved his work! It was no wonder he whistled.

"Grandpa," asked Susie, one day, "when Sophie and I grow up and marry and have homes of our own, will thee make chairs and tables for us?"

"God willing," answered Grandpa, whistling gaily. "But if thee is patient and bides thy time, Susie, and thee also, Sophie, p'raps you won't be obliged to wait so long for

something clever from the shop of your Grandpa Gooding."

At that, Susie and Sophie fairly fluttered around Grandpa's shop.

"Will it be a doll's cradle, Grandpa?" asked Susie, and her voice rang like a chime of high-pitched bells.

"Grandpa, will it be a little desk, with pigeon-holes, and drawers, and real glass doors?" asked Sophie, and her dimple danced in her cheek.

"Will it be a teeny-weeny pie-crust table, Grandpa, where we can play at having little dinners with our china tea-set?" asked Susie, her breath coming quick.

"Oh, Grandpa, *what* will it be?" cried Sophie.

"And *when*, Grandpa?" begged Susie.

Grandpa twinkled at them. "A secret bides its time until the right moment comes," he answered. "And maybe the right moment will come on a birthday—a double birthday such as twins have.

"Maybe," added Grandpa, mysteriously.

THE THIRD CHAPTER

The twins' seventh birthday seemed a long way off. They counted, and found they had four months and nine days to wait. But there is one sure thing about Time. It's bound to travel steadily along, quite slowly for girls and boys, faster for their parents, and very fast indeed for their grandpas.

The rest of Sixth Month traveled steadily

along. Seventh Month spun out its thirty-one days. Eighth Month did the same. Ninth Month did not skip a single day. But now Sophie and Susie knew that *something* was in Grandpa Gooding's shop which had not been there when he first said that a secret bides its time.

So every day the twins paid a visit to the shop. Every day, sizzling with whispers, they paused outside the door. They cleared their throats politely, but loud a-plenty. They scuffed their feet against the step. They rattled the latch, softly. Any kind of a *mannerly* sound would do. Just so their dear grandpa was sure to hear them!

He always did. From inside the shop, there would come sly, scurrying noises, as he hastened to cover up the Secret. Then,

stillness. Suddenly, Grandpa would begin to whistle his loudest. That was a sign he was ready. Holding their breath, the twins would tiptoe quickly over the threshold, pretending not to be looking for anything special. But every time, their bright glances, swift as birds, flew to the queer, humpy shape of the Secret, hidden under an old blue coverlet.

Tenth Month arrived. And after it had spun out eleven slow days, it suddenly presented the twins with a jolly gift of Time's own—their seventh birthday.

"But it's raining buckets!" fretted Susie.

"On our birthday!" sighed Sophie.

And they wondered if Grandpa Gooding were quite ready. If so, how could he ever carry the Secret from shop to house without

getting it wet? And when? After school? How could they wait so many, many hours? Oh, if only they weren't obliged to go to school on their seventh birthday!

Grandpa Gooding walked over and stood by the kitchen window. He stared out at the pouring rain. "I doubt if there's been a wetter day since the Flood," he remarked. "At least a wetter *birth*day," he added, rolling his eyes toward the twins.

Then Grandpa crossed the room and looked through the opposite window. "I declare, it seems even wetter on this side!" he exclaimed. "Noah would never have sent his twin grand-daughters to school in such a rain as this!"

Rachel Gooding, the twins' mother, laughed. "It does seem as if the rain had set

in for the day," she agreed. "I think Sophie and Susie might stay at home."

"Did you hear that?" whispered Sophie to Susie.

"Oh, yes!" whispered Susie to Sophie. And they thought they had never seen a lovelier rain.

Grandpa lifted his oldest hat from the hook behind the kitchen door. He pulled on his boots. He put on his greatcoat, not his best one. He went outside, whistling. The twins watched him splashing along the path until he reached his shop. Then they skittered away and hid in the tall clothes-press, for it would never, never do even to peep at the Secret before the right moment came. Among the cloaks and shawls Susie and Sophie listened, shivering and giggling.

At last they heard the outer door close. Grandpa was whistling as never before. They heard a thump. "Sophie! Susie! Come, now! It is exactly the right moment!" called Grandpa.

The clothes-press shook as the twins plunged out of it. They stopped short, for at that very moment Grandpa whisked the blue coverlet, dripping with rain, off the Secret. And there, rocking gently in the middle of the kitchen floor, was the cleverest, the most charming little chair! The twins stared and stared, for they had never seen anything like it in all their seven years.

"A double rocker, for twins!" cried Mother, laughing. And she lifted the lid of the ingle-nook seat, and tossed out a pair of gay cushions which she had been making as

a surprise of her own. The cushions were of red calico, sprinkled over with tiny yellow rosebuds. Ruffled all around. Pretty as twin posy-beds. Mother tied a cushion in each chair.

"Try the rocker now, Grand-daughters," urged Grandpa.

Carefully the twins eased themselves into it. Sophie touched her toes to the floor and gave her body a slight push forward. The chair began to rock. *Stars-to-goodness,* when Sophie rocked forward, Susie rocked backward! *Laws-a-mighty,* when Susie's toes pointed toward the ceiling, Sophie's toes brushed the floor! Each had a chair of her own, yet they rocked in the same chair. The wonder of it was scarcely to be believed. For Grandpa, from a supply of sturdy hick-

ory wood, had first built two chairs exactly alike. Then, as if the chairs were also loving twin sisters, he had linked the left arm of one with the right arm of the other. They made a double rocker, side by side, but facing opposite. Only a grandpa who loved his work and whistled all the while could have made such a clever piece of furniture. Only a grandpa who loved his twin grand-daughters could ever have planned such a wonderful birthday present.

Now on the bare boards of the kitchen floor the rockers made a contented, home-y rhythm as Sophie and Susie swayed back and forth, back and forth. Their cheeks were as red as the cushions. Their pigtails flew out behind them. Sophie's dimple danced in her cheek. Susie's eyes shone bright as

22

lighted candles. Oh, it was a birthday that *rocked* with fun, and with pride in the charming twin rocker.

"Thee is the best grandpa in all the wide world!" cried Sophie and Susie.

"You are uncommonly good granddaughters yourselves," said Grandpa. And while they rocked with might and main, he whistled his merriest.

THE FOURTH CHAPTER

In the happy weeks that followed, Sophie and Susie Gooding seemed never to tire of their double rocking-chair. They rocked themselves by the hour. They rocked their twin dolls. Every small thing that was most precious to them, they rocked in their precious new chair. They studied their lessons in it. They played guessing games and riddles in it. And sometimes they sat quietly, without rocking, and sewed on their patchwork. They were making "Ocean Wave" quilts. Sophie's was pink-

26

and-white. Susie's was blue-and-white. They expected to have them finished by the time they were seventeen, when two nice young Quaker gentlemen would undoubtedly come along and ask to marry them.

Susie could sew a shade more neatly than Sophie. Perhaps, though one could only guess, it was because Susie had no dimple in her cheek.

Mother was happy to see how contentedly, how merrily, her twin daughters rocked in the double chair. And Grandpa! Why, Grandpa Gooding had never whistled with more vim. Several times he came within a chirrup of whistling a real tune!

The neighbors, far and near, heard of the chair. They dropped in to see it. The grown-ups were quick with praise for Grandpa. "Thee has turned out a very

clever piece of handiwork, Friend Gooding," they said. And the eyes of the little Quaker children were as round as buttons when they saw the pretty rocker with its gay twin cushions. "I would admire to have a chair like that," said seven-year-old Delphina Shaw, who lived a mile or so down the road. "Me, too," lisped her six-year-old sister, Mercy Shaw.

The cold, cloudy days of Eleventh Month slipped away, one by one. Twelfth Month brought sleet and snow. But inside the house where Susie and Sophie Gooding lived, there was warm firelight, and happy laughter, and Grandpa's jaunty whistling. And there was the contented rocking, to and fro, of the little twin rocker.

THE FIFTH CHAPTER

irst Month brought a new year. But it brought something else new and strange. All of a sudden Susie and Sophie Gooding began to tease and torment each other. Not in fun, either.

Sophie started it. Why? No one could guess. Perhaps it was because she had eaten too many pancakes for breakfast. Or, perhaps it was just one of those cross, cranky mornings that sometimes pop up the minute one jumps out of bed. For of course one

wouldn't want to believe it was because Sophie had a dimple in her cheek!

At any rate, it happened on Seventh Day, which you may perhaps call Saturday. It should always be one of the very best days of the week, as every one knows.

The twins were rocking high, wide, and handsome. Suddenly, without the least warning, Sophie planted her square-toed shoes squarely on the floor. It was a tricky, unfair thing to do. It stopped the chair, short. Poor Susie almost tumbled out on her nose. When she tried to rock again, what did Sophie do but bring the chair to another sudden standstill!

Susie glanced quickly at her twin. Sophie's dimple was nowhere in sight. She had a naughty glint in her eye, and she

looked as disagreeable as if her name had been Sophie Sauce-box.

Susie wasn't used to such looks, nor such behavior. Her own temper flared up quick as tinder. The next instant she let fly and knocked Sophie's elbow off the middle arm of the chair.

Sophie knocked Susie's elbow—*thump!* She began rocking like fury. It was Susie, then, who planted her feet on the floor— *Snap!*

"Now, this is a fine pickle!" cried Mother. "Whatever in the world ails you, Sophie and Susie Gooding?"

And Grandpa stopped whistling. He stared at his grand-daughters as if he could not believe his eyes. Nor his ears, either.

Indeed, it was quite impossible to believe

that loving twin sisters who had never quarreled, could so misbehave. Especially in the pretty twin chair that was so precious to them.

But that was only the beginning of the teasing and tormenting. They began again on Second Day, if you can believe it! They thought up sly new schemes for vexing one another. Even when they sewed on their quilts, Sophie would jog Susie's elbow. Or, Susie would jog, rudely. The long, crooked stitches in the "Ocean Wave" quilts were a sight to behold.

"Alas!" sighed Mother. "I would be ashamed for any young Quaker gentlemen to see such higgledy-piggledy needlework! Indeed, Twins, I doubt if you will ever get yourselves husbands!"

Lackadaisy! Sophie and Susie felt quite faint with alarm. But in spite of such a dreadful possibility, the next moment they had completely forgotten how important husbands might some day be.

Once more, then, the twins fell to squabbling and scowling.

Grandpa leaned toward Mother. In a low, solemn voice he said, "Has thee noticed, Rachel, that Susie and Sophie now look precisely alike? Which is Susie? And which is Sophie?" asked Grandpa.

Mother gazed at the twins, while they hung their heads and blushed as red as beets. "It is true, Grandpa," she whispered at last. "The dimple in Sophie's cheek has been gone for a week of days. It's an odd thing about a dimple, Grandpa," Mother went on.

37

"It doesn't show itself in a little girl's cheek unless she is happy and smiling. And without Sophie's dimple how can we tell the children apart?"

So that was now the dismal state of affairs in the house where those Gooding twins lived. The fire crackled on the hearth just the same. But there was no sound of happy laughter. Instead of the contented, home-y rhythm of the rockers on the kitchen floor, there were only sudden jerks and thumps, most ugly and unpleasant.

And Grandpa Gooding had stopped whistling. Days went by, and not a single chirrup came from Grandpa's lips.

"Why doesn't thee whistle as thee used to, Grandpa?" asked Susie, although deep in her heart she knew well enough.

"Why not, Grandpa?" asked Sophie.
She knew also, the baggage!

Grandpa's mouth was straight and stern
as he answered, "It's because of my twin

grand-daughters. 'T isn't every grandpa has such naughty ones."

Sophie and Susie could have sunk through the floor with shame. For an hour or two they were quite well-behaved. Then, *lacka-daisy*, the teasing and tormenting began again!

But don't think for one instant that Sophie and Susie Gooding were happy, being such unmannerly little snippets! Why, they ached from head to toe with the misery of being naughty!

There is no misery any worse than that!

THE SIXTH CHAPTER

At last one day Mother said something that made the twins' hearts stand still. And the little hickory chair seemed to freeze in its tracks. It stopped rocking. It made no more noise than a broken clock.

"Grandpa," said Mother, "I think thee had better put on thy boots and greatcoat and go down the road a mile or so to the

house of Neighbor Shaw. Ask him and his good wife Rebecca if they would like to buy the double rocking-chair. I feel sure that Mercy and Delphina Shaw would greatly admire to have such a clever toy. Thee could ask as handsome a price as thee's a mind to, for thee put all thy love and fine skill into its making, and there is not another like it anywhere."

"Very well, Rachel," agreed Grandpa, gravely. And he sat down by the fire and began pulling on his left boot.

Sophie's and Susie's eyes were the size of saucers. Both little girls bounced out of the chair so suddenly that it started to rocking. It kept on rocking, all by itself. "Oh-h-h! Oh-h-h!" The little chair seemed to be moaning in pain.

And Susie and Sophie cried out, "Mother!

Thee can't mean *our* rocking-chair! Grandpa, NO! Mercy and Delphina are not twins, Grandpa. And it's a twin chair thee made 'specially for thy own twin grand-daughters."

Grandpa didn't say a word. He pulled on his right boot.

"Your poor grandpa scarcely knows you any more," explained Mother, sadly. "Nor does he know for sure which is Susie and which is Sophie. He can't see you behind your scowls and frowns. He can't hear the pleasant sounds of home for the din of your quarreling. And since you have quarreled only since the twin rocker joined our fireside, it must be that you no longer like it. Such a pretty thing to say farewell to forever," added Mother.

"We do like our little hickory chair," said Sophie, in a very low voice. She hung her head. Her lips quivered.

"It was never the fault of the nice little rocking-chair," said Susie, and her voice

44

could scarcely be heard. Her chin shook.

Grandpa and Mother looked at each other, their eyes brightening. Oh, *heavenly day,* were Sophie and Susie going to be good girls, after all?

But just as such a thing seemed possible, Susie flipped her skirt and tossed her head, and her eyes flashed with anger. "It was

Sophie started the teasing and tormenting," she cried.

"It was Susie kept it up, and kept it up," cried Sophie. And she stamped her foot as no little Quaker girl was ever known to do.

Mother turned away, disappointed.

With a long sigh, Grandpa lifted his greatcoat from the hook. "Rachel, I think I shall not go to Neighbor Shaw's," he said, quietly. "Since Sophie and Susie no longer love each other, they should have *separate* chairs. I'll attend to it." And he went out the door.

Oh, what was Grandpa going to do next? The twins watched him trudge grimly along the snowy path toward his workshop. Then Sophie ran, trembling, and hid behind the kitchen dresser. Susie hid, shaking and aching, in the tall clothes-press. The house

was very still, while they waited.

Presently they heard the outer door open,
and close. They heard Grandpa stalk into
the kitchen. Slowly, feebly, they crept from
their hiding-places.

THE LAST CHAPTER

Grandpa had brought a tool from his workshop. It had a wooden handhold, and a broad, shining blade. The blade was edged with a row of sharp, grinning teeth. It appeared to be the very thing it was—a handsaw.

"Grandpa!" cried Sophie, and she shivered and shook.

"Grandpa!" wailed Susie, and the cold chills raced down her spine like a parade of swift little spiders.

Grandpa behaved as if he didn't hear. He acted as if there were no little girls within a mile of him. Very carefully he set the teeth of the saw against the place where one chair linked its arm so prettily with the arm of its twin.

"Such a pity! Such a sorry pity!" murmured Mother.

Susie snatched at Grandpa's coat-tail. "Oh, please, Grandpa, don't, DON'T!"

Sophie snatched at the other coat-tail. "Please, Grandpa, you *wouldn't* saw the little double chair in two!"

But Grandpa sawed steadily up and down, up and down. There were harsh, grating

sounds, and a tiny chip of wood flew from the hickory chair.

"Oh me, oh my!" Susie and Sophie could not bear to watch the ruin of their dearest toy. Howling with grief, they threw their arms around each other. Sophie hid her eyes against Susie's shoulder. Her tears rained down on Susie's left pigtail. Susie's tears dripped off Sophie's left pigtail. They clutched each other in wild despair.

And all the while the sharp-toothed saw flashed rapidly back and forth. But if the twins had not been howling and wailing so loud, they might have noticed that the saw made almost no noise. And that no more chips flew, either.

Just as they were expecting to hear the awful clatter of the double chair falling

apart, Mother cried out, "Grandpa! It appears to me that Sophie and Susie may really love each other, after all. Perhaps thee had better stop thy work long enough to look at them."

Grandpa stopped sawing. He peered intently at his weeping grand-daughters. "Why, bless my soul!" he exclaimed. "They are hanging one to the other like— well, like twin sisters who love each other."

"We do l-l-love each other," sobbed the twins. "And we d-d-dote on our little chair." Sophie took a careful peep around Susie's wilted shoulder ruffle. Susie opened one eye, the merest squint. And what did they see?

Why, the double rocking-chair was as whole and pretty as ever it had been, except

for a tiny white nick where Grandpa had first started to saw it in two. *Joy!* Susie rushed for one chair. Sophie rushed for the other. They began to rock. They rocked high. They rocked low. Their pigtails flew out behind them. Their cheeks glowed as red as the cushions on which they sat. Sophie's dimple danced in her cheek. Susie's eyes shone bright as lighted candles.

"There is Sophie!" cried Mother, pointing.

"So the other one is Susie," said Grandpa. Smiling, he sat down by the fire and pulled off his boots. He began to whistle. He whistled as he had never whistled in all his born days.

"What a pretty, pretty tune, dear Grandpa!" cooed Sophie and Susie.

And that was the last, the very last, of the teasing and the tormenting and the quarreling. Within the house where Susie and Sophie lived, there was ever the sound of happy laughter, and of Grandpa's cheerful whistling. And so long as the twins were young, there was the home-y, contented rhythm, to and fro, of the charming twin rocker.